Walt Disney's
SANTA'S TOY SHOP

ILLUSTRATIONS BY
THE WALT DISNEY STUDIO
ADAPTED BY AL DEMPSTER

A GOLDEN BOOK • NEW YORK
Western Publishing Company, Inc.
Racine, Wisconsin 53404

Western Publishing Company, Inc.
offers a wide variety of children's
videos, tapes and games.

For information write to:
    Western Publishing Company, Inc.
    1220 Mound Avenue
    Racine, WI 53404

This Little Golden Book was produced under the supervision of

THE WALT DISNEY STUDIO

WAY UP NORTH in the land of ice and snow stands a cozy little house. And beside the front door hangs a neat little sign. *S. Claus*, says the sign. Because that is who lives there—Santa Claus.

Mrs. Santa Claus lives there, too, of course.
She keeps house for Santa Claus, and for all
the elves who work in Santa's toy shop.
And what a busy place that toy shop is!

In the doll department. . .

and the train department...

and the game and building set department. . .

and dozens of departments up and down the halls, happy little Christmas elves are busy all year long, making and trying out the toys.

Oh, everyone is busy in Santa's toy shop.
But Santa Claus is busiest of all. He shows
the doll makers how to paint on smiles.

"I'll take a day off soon," says Santa Claus, "and play!"

But letters keep coming from boys and girls, wanting talking dolls and cowboy boots, rocking horses and fireman suits.

"I'm just *too* busy!" Santa Claus sometimes says. "I never have time to play with the toys."

And most of those children have been so good, Santa has to do his best to please them.

So the days whiz by in Santa's toy shop. And soon it is Christmas Eve again. And Santa Claus has still not played with a single toy!

"Oh, jumping jacks!" said Santa Claus last Christmas Eve, as Mrs. Claus buttoned up his warm red coat: "Now I have to give all these toys away, and I never will get to try any out!" And he almost scowled.

But Mrs. Claus whispered something into Santa's ear, and he left the house chuckling to himself.

"Wonderful idea!" the reindeer heard him say, as they waited at the door, hitched to the heaped-up sleigh.

Then all night long around the world they
flew. And Santa dropped down chimneys

with his load of toys, or slipped in doors or
windows, where the chimney didn't fit.

The load grew lighter in the sleigh as they went. And at last Santa Claus was slipping down the chimney into the very last house on his list.

There he found a Christmas tree all set up.
And he put the final touches on it, and lit all
the lights.

He found a plate of cookies and a glass of milk, with a note that said, "For Dear Santa Claus." So he sat himself down and had a bite of lunch.

Then he unpacked the toys, as he always does. But he did not hustle right away. Not this time. No!

He set up the new electric train and sent
it speeding around the track and through
the tunnel.

He sent the model airplane spinning
around the Christmas tree. And he built a
whole village with Christmas blocks.

When Santa had tried every Christmas
toy, back home he flew in his magical sleigh
to Mrs. Santa Claus.

"Never have I had such fun," Santa told Mrs. Santa Claus. "I did as you suggested and stopped at the last house." And he whispered the children's names in her ear.

Do you think he might pick your house to stop at this year?